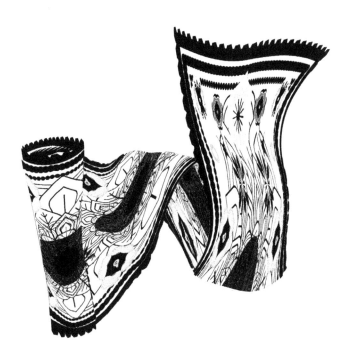

Other books by
Kristina Murray-Hally

Max's Magnificent Glasses
Captain Loose Tooth
The Very Long Sausage Dog
The Great Bookworm
Monster Spray
George's Gigantic Telescope

Miss Silverstein

Kristina Murray-Hally

Illustrated by Hanlik Arts

First published in Australia by Spiders 8 Media

Postal: PO BOX 2379 East Ivanhoe Vic 3079

Email: murrayhally@gmail.com

Website: www.kristinamurray-hally.com

Copyright ©2019 Kristina Murray-Hally

National Library of Australia Cataloguing–in–Publication entry

Creator: Murray-Hally, Kristina, author.

Title: Miss Silverstein / Kristina Murray-Hally; Hanlik Arts, illustrator.

ISBN: 978-0-9942738-5-7 (paperback)

ISBN: 978-0-6487072-5-7 (epub)

Printed by Ingram Spark

To Theadora and Seraphina
May your love of learning take you to
amazing places.

Chapter One

It was the first day of third grade when Sophie and her friends saw their new teacher, Miss Silverstein. Tall, thin, and with long brown hair, she wore a skirt and pale pink cardigan. Over her shoulder she carried a bag, and under her arm, what looked like a rolled-up carpet.

Miss Silverstein had a skip in her step as she entered the school office building.

"There she is! I think that is Miss Silverstein!" said Sophie to her friends Sophie thought her new teacher seemed nice and was excited to meet her.

The bell rang and Sophie and her friends ran to their new classroom. There stood a happy and smiling Miss Silverstein, waiting at the door.

"Good morning," she said with warmth that felt like sunshine. "I'm looking for two straight lines and then we'll go inside," said Miss Silverstein with a sweet voice.

The class filed into the room. Miss Silverstein

had decorated it with bright posters and a vibrant new rug. The rug was beautiful, made up of a pink, orange and yellow colour palate. On this eye-catching background were well-known landmarks that looked like they had been sketched lightly using grey lead pencil.

"Look at that! The Taj Mahal," pointed William.

"There is the Great Wall of China," added Harriet excitedly.

Looking very closely at the Great Pyramids were Samuel and Louis. There were screams of delight as Isobel and Sophie called out, "the Statue of Liberty!"

Sophie and her classmates couldn't stop looking at the rug.

"Children, please sit down next to your bags," she said, and waited for them all to be seated on the rug. "Good morning and welcome to Grade 3S. My name is Miss Silverstein and I will be your teacher this year," she said smiling.

"As you can see, you are sitting on my amazing rug, and its name is Tappeto. He comes with me wherever I am teaching." Tappeto suddenly started to move, rising slightly up from the floor.

"We are moving!" gasped Jonathan.

"Oh WOW!" said Isobel.

"This is like being on a hovercraft!" said Sophie.

"I can't touch the floor!" said William looking over the edge.

Miss Silverstein waved her hand at Tappeto and suddenly the rug settled back on the floor.

Sophie and the other children looked at their new teacher, smiles wide and their eyes gleaming with amazement at Miss Silverstein and Tappeto, her extraordinary rug.

Chapter Two

Over the next few weeks Tappeto was mostly a normal floor rug. Occasionally, the class would see him move or roll himself up, and the children were always on the look out to see what Tappeto might do next.

The real insight into the extent of the magic of the magnificent floor rug came on the morning of their school camp.

It was a busy morning as the children and the parent helpers assembled in Sophie's classroom. "Girls and boys please sit down," said Miss Silverstein, who then took the class roll and explained the safety issues. The class was so excited that they were moving about, talking and laughing.

Suddenly, the door shook so loudly as Mrs Bombardo, the school principal, marched in.

Mrs Bombardo was a short, solid woman with spiky dyed-brown hair. She ran the school like an army officer.

"ATTENTION!" she yelled with a voice

that sounded like an angry guard dog. The class and Miss Silverstein stopped and turned to look at Mrs Bombardo. Nobody moved.

"GOOD morning! All ready for camp? Listen to your teacher and parent-helpers," she said like a sergeant giving her soldiers orders. With that she abruptly turned around with the precision of a marching band and left the classroom.

As she closed the door behind her she could hear noises of cheering and happiness. The corridor walls started to shake. She stopped. Her beady snake-like eyes turned to stare at Miss Silverstein's classroom door.

I knew I should never have employed her... too nice, not cruel enough, she thought to herself. More screams of delight that sounded like children on a fair ride, rang through Mrs Bombardo's ears as she opened the door.

Shock! Horror! Mrs Bombardo thought as she stepped into the classroom again and saw all the children laughing and talking on a moving floor rug – Tappeto. With a *WOOSH*, the beautiful rug with the children, Miss Silverstein and parent-helpers aboard, suddenly moved towards the large open window.

"STOP! STOP! STOP!" screamed Mrs Bombardo. "You don't have my permission!"

She ran to catch the rug, and managed to grasp the tassels. It was a sight to see a class of children staring at a screaming principal hanging on to the edge of a flying carpet! Mrs Bombardo looked like a witch who had lost her broom and was being rescued by people on a flying carpet!

Miss Silverstein and the parent-helpers pulled Mrs Bombardo up onto the rug, like a group of sailors pulling up a huge and heavy anchor!

Mrs Bombardo was so exhausted and in shock she didn't say a word. Being scared of heights as she was, she didn't move either. She rested for the remainder of the trip, eyes tightly closed.

Chapter Three

They had been travelling for a few hours and the scenery had changed.

"We are getting closer to the Amazon rainforest," said Miss Silverstein.

There was land and mountains to the far left and to the right they could see the ocean. Tappeto turned in the direction of the mountains.

"Look at all of those trees! It looks like a big, green carpet!" said Charlotte. The children moved to the edge of Tappeto.

"All the green you can see below us is known as a canopy, a tree canopy. The canopy layer is teeming with life as it is rich in fruits and seeds. Animals such as insects, birds, monkeys, frogs and sloths are found here. It is said the canopy layer is home to ninety percent of animals in the rainforest," [1, para. 3] Miss Silverstein explained.

"Plants are found in the canopy, growing layer on the lofty tree branches, without roots in the soil below. These are called 'air plants' because they can make their own food just using sunlight and the nutrients taken from the air and water dripping onto their leaves," [2, para. 4] said Miss Silverstein.

The group was mesmerised by Miss Silverstein's knowledge.

The children had noticed the weather had changed, too. When they had left the school it was grey and over-cast, now it was sunny and humid, like being in a butterfly enclosure at the zoo. The children took off their jumpers and put on their hats.

This would be a great opportunity to speak to the children some more about the Amazon rainforest, thought Miss Silverstein and with that thought something unexpected happened...

Tappeto extended, like the red carpet being rolled out for a special event and then section of it moved up quickly towards the sky - it now looked like a carpet wall hanging! Tappeto was now shaped like the capital letter 'L'. The design on the top end of the rug had faded and had become a whiteboard with the heading at the top that read, 'Amazon Rainforest'.

As Miss Silverstein spoke dot points appeared with the important points she was making. Some children were finding this to be so magical, it is possible they weren't listening to everything Miss Silverstein said.

"How did this happen?" asked William carefully craning his neck to have a look and see what may have been behind the 'whiteboard'. There was nothing there; it just looked like the back of a normal floor rug.

"I will answer your question a bit later," said Miss Silverstein.

As if there had been no interruption, Miss Silverstein continued... "The Amazon is the world's largest tropical rainforest. Covering over 5.5 million square kilometres, it's so big that the United Kingdom and Ireland would fit into it 17 times!" [3, para. 2].

The children listened intently.

"The Amazon is found in South America, spanning across Brazil, Bolivia, Peru, Ecuador, Colombia, Venezuela, Guyana, Suriname and French Guiana" [4, para. 3].

"We will be staying in Brazil near Manaus," added Miss Silverstein.

"How long is the Amazon River?" asked Charlotte.

"It runs through the north of the rainforest, it flows the length of around 6,400km!" [5].

"The Amazon has an incredibly rich ecosystem – there are around 40,000 plant species, 1,300 bird species, 3,000 types of fish, 430 mammals and a whopping 2.5 million different insects" [6, para. 7].

"WOW!" the students replied in unison.

The children asked Miss Silverstein some interesting questions: "What is the largest predator in the Amazon?" asked Samuel and "Is it true that there are pink river dolphins?" asked Isobel. Without thinking Miss Silverstein answered their questions and then the dot points disappeared and the whiteboard slide back into the edge of Tappeto. They could now feel Tappeto moving steadily downwards.

"Children, Tappeto has started our descent. Please pack up your board games and lunch boxes," said Miss Silverstein.

They were excited as they hurried to organise themselves.

Chapter Four

It was only a few minutes before the class saw the clearing where Tappeto was going to land.

"As we prepare for landing please sit up straight, have your bags in front of you and hold onto the tassels until after we have landed," said Miss Silverstein like an air steward's safety announcement.

The air blew through their hair as Tappeto picked up speed. It was a smooth and swift arrival, more like a bird swooping down and landing on a patch of lawn.

As Mrs Bombardo stepped onto the grass, she started her barrage of requests. "Miss Silverstein where are we? Explain this mode of transport? Where are the permission forms? The parents thought the children were travelling on a bus and then a plane! How will you explain this?" she screeched.

"Meet Tappeto, my friend and flying carpet," said Miss Silverstein.

"We could say it is a different version of a

plane," said Harriet's mum.

"It was an amazing experience flying over the ocean!" added William's dad.

For once Mrs Bombardo was left without words. As they trailed off into the nearby forest. Mrs Bombardo walked behind the class with what looked like steam coming out of her ears!

It was hot and humid and the damp grass came up past their knees.

"I can't see my shoes!" said Leonardo.

They tried to keep a forward gaze so as to distract them from what might lay beneath the long, thin blades of grass. It wasn't long before they could see some huts - wooden structures with thatched roofs. The huts were randomly situated along the river bank.

"Children, we are here in the Amazon rainforest. This will be a wonderful learning experience for all of us. I will divide you into groups, and a parent-helper will be your group leader. For the rest of the trip you will need to stay closely with your group and listen carefully to your leader," Miss Silverstein said. "We are now in an environment that we will share with other creatures, including ...electric eels, flesh eating piranhas, poison dart frogs, jaguars and some seriously venomous snakes" [7, para. 8].

There are also other humans... so it is an amazing place but it also holds many dangers!" said Miss Silverstein.

"It is DANGEROUS!" screamed Mrs Bombardo throwing herself to the ground. "ARRG! It is a slimy FROG!"As patient and understanding as Miss Silverstein was, Mrs Bombardo was now beginning to stretch Miss Silverstein's tolerance.

With that Mrs Bombardo ran to stand directly behind Miss Silverstein and the children followed their parent-helper to their huts.

"This is our hut!" said William. As he opened the door it smelt musty and of old wet wood. It was dark and through the slates he could see daylight.

"Did you hear that?" remarked Harriet. There was sure to be small animals that had made their homes in their roof, she thought.

The children couldn't see anything as they unpacked their bags.

After they had settled in they had some free time to play and run around, meanwhile the parent-helpers organised dinner.

The children were hungry and they gobbled down their food and the group rostered on to wash and clean up did so. Then it was time to get ready for bed. There was a lot of rambunctious noise trying to get the sixteen children organised and settled in their hammocks. "Look at me!" said Leonardo swinging his hammock from side to side. It was such a novelty for them to be sleeping in hammocks that it took extra time to quiet them down.

*   *   *

It was just as the sun rose that Mrs Bombardo woke up and came out of her hut.

"How did you sleep?" asked Harriet's mum.

"I had the most restful sleep in a long time... it's the most comfortable bed I have ever slept on. It felt like sleeping on a large plate of soft moving jelly."

"Did you say MOVING?"asked Harriet's mum.

"YES!" replied Mrs Bombardo.

"It is moving! Your SNAKE SKIN patterned blanket is MOVING... outside of your HUT!" said Harriet's mum.

In minutes the entire camp site, the nocturnal animals, and anybody within cooee of Mrs Bombardo were woken by an enormous scream – it's an ANACONDA!

"What is all the commotion?" asked Miss Silverstein as she emerged from her hut.

"Mrs Bombardo slept on an ANACONDA!"

Some of the children were laughing; some screaming and others just smiled.

"This place isn't SAFE!" Mrs Bombardo yelled.

The yelling scared the snake back into the river.

Chapter Five

Everyone in the campsite turned to movement in the nearby forest. A group of natives in traditional dress fanned out around the clearing.

"*Ah Buk Ak Bhar Har.* We have come to see what all the noise is about," stated the Chief of the Hermities – the clan of the Great Jaguar Warriors who was holding a long sharp stick.

"Who are you? What brings you to our land?" asked the tribesman, his traditional dress consisting of a skirt made from some long leaves and many colourful beaded necklaces hung around his neck. His face and chest were painted with lines like all the other tribes people, had dots across their noses then up alone their nose forming a 'Y' shape. The patterns were painted in black, red and brown.

The children scattered; some of them ran into their huts, some hid behind trees and some ran and tried to hide behind Miss Silverstein and the parent-helpers.

"What are you doing on our land?" This

time the chief said it in a louder voice and banged his stick on the ground.

Miss Silverstein was fluent in their language and translated it to her class as he spoke.

"Let me introduce myself," said Miss Silverstein stepping forward to meet the chief. She held out her hand with great confidence in the hope that he would shake her hand.

He did, and then issued orders to his tribesman in his own language. They all put down their sharp sticks.

Miss Silverstein explained the situation and apologised for the noise and disruption. The clan members walked around the camp site looking at everything.

"We thought that this was a public recreation village for school groups?" said Miss Silverstein as she followed the chief.

"This is our land and the huts belong to us!" he said.

Mrs Bombardo, who was returning from the bathroom, suddenly dropped her toiletry bag and began screaming.

"Take me HOME! NOW!" she bellowed, her face turning bright red like an over-ripe tomato.

"We'll take her with us," said one of the tribesmen and they dragged her off kicking and yelling.

"What are you doing? Where are you taking her?" asked Miss Silverstein.

"She'll be right!" said one of the tribesmen. "We will bring her back by sunset," he added. They carried her away like a lumber jack carrying a fallen log.

Miss Silverstein smirked as she thought about Mrs Bombardo's bad behaviour. Then a rush of seriousness flooded her thinking... *We need to find her and bring her back to school... in one piece!*

"She is the school principal and we can't let a group of Amazon natives take off with her, she may be in great danger," said Miss Silverstein.

"I'm sure she can defend herself," said Isobel's mum.

As the tribesmen walked away, the volume

of Mrs Bombardo's screaming became fainter and fainter, until all that could be heard were birds in nearby trees.

"That was crazy!" said William.

"Hopefully they return her or I will have a lot of explaining to do," said Miss Silverstein to the parent- helpers.

"Let's remain calm. We will work on a solution! They look serious but I think they will look after Mrs Bombardo."

Chapter Six

"Before we follow them I wanted to let you know that it's believed that about fifty of the indigenous Amerindian tribes who live in the Amazon rainforest have never had contact with the outside world!" [8, p.45] explained Miss Silverstein.

The class smiled, enjoying all the knowledge their teacher was providing.

"Let's go and find out more!" whispered Miss Silverstein to Tappeto. "Quietly everyone," said Miss Silverstein as she motioned for the group to sit on Tappeto.

With everyone aboard the flying carpet, very quickly they were up and away when Sophie spotted the tribes-people.

Tappeto and his passengers hid in a large tree where they all had a bird's-eye view of what was happening. It seemed quite busy with many tribes-people moving around - cooking, building, and children playing.

But there was no sign of Mrs Bombardo.

Tappeto moved from tree to tree to try to get a better look. As they were all starting to weary, out of the corner of Sophie's eye she saw her principal sitting on a log.

Suddenly the sides of Tappeto curled up around the class like a tunnel; it now felt like they were in a plane. A few of the students tried to move and it seemed that they were glued to the rug! In no time at all Tappeto was performing manoeuvres like a fighter pilot.

The reverse side of Tappeto has an invisibility function where it couldn't be seen. The threads of the rug activated a magical effect that made Tappeto completely impossible to see.

They were so close they could hear the conversation.

"Drink this juice," demanded one of the tribesmen thrusting a cup towards the principal.

"I am not going to drink it; it could be poison for all I know!"

"You need to drink it as it will make you feel much better, and you will begin to feel and behave like a nice human being rather than an angry lion!"

"What do you mean?"

"We can see from your eyes and voice you are lacking some special gifts such as kindness, understanding, patience and love."

"Well that's not working," said the largest tribesman to the one standing next to him.
"Right then, we'll send her further into the jungle, and there she will learn the traits she needs!"

"The spirit of the wild animals will teach her a thing or two," said another tribesman.

"The wind has told us that you need to learn a few things... so we will send you into the jungle for three days and three nights," said the chief.

Mrs Bombardo couldn't believe her ears. She was used to making the demands and having others follow the rules.

"I'M NOT MOVING!" she yelled and with that the tribes-people picked her up and carried her further into the jungle.

They found a large tree and left her with an emergency leaf whistle. "Blow this when you think you are ready to return. You will know when the green spirits have spoken," explained one of the tribes-people.

They quickly ran off, leaving Mrs Bombardo alone and trying desperately to use her new leaf whistle that didn't seem to work.

Chapter Seven

Tappeto reversed the invisibility function and flew like a fighter jet on an angle again and landed in a clearing between some trees. Miss Silverstein and her group moved off Tappeto and sat on a rock wondering what to do next.

Tappeto rolled himself up much like a newspaper ready to be placed in a round letterbox. Miss Silverstein picked up Tappeto and kept him near her like you would a pet. Together they were thinking about what to do next when they were interrupted by a group of people from the Hermities Tribe.

"We are one of the oldest tribes of the Amazon. What brings you to our land, the land of the green spirits?" asked an elderly grandmother figure. "My name is Xoana, the ancient grandmother of the Hermities.

Her face appeared to be like thick leather, weathered by the sun. Her eyes, an incredible hazel colour, glistened like the muddy waters of the nearby river.

Miss Silverstein stepped forward and confidently said "Nice to meet you, Xoana. My name is Miss Silverstein and this is my third-grade class. We are on a school camp and the school principal, Mrs Bombardo has unfortunately brought a lot of attention to herself and our school group."

She gave Xoana a smile then continued, "Sorry, we didn't know it was the Hermities' home and the land of the green spirits. We also apologise for the noise and disruption to the jungle and all who live here. We would greatly appreciate your help with finding our principal. She will be very angry and we last saw her being carried off by some tribesmen." Miss Silverstein smiled again then returned to stand beside Sophie's dad.

"Thank you for the explanation," said Xoana. "We welcome you with open arms and hearts. Anything new causes my people to become concerned. I will send a flock of birds to ask for her return," explained the grandmother figure.

She then invited Miss Silverstein and her

group -including Tappeto - to share some food with her people while they awaited the return of Mrs Bombardo.

Chapter Eight

Miss Silverstein and her group followed Xoana back to the Hermities home and sipped cups of sugary coffee and tasted some food. The other tribes-people didn't say a word, just watched what was going on.

"Please come with me for some lunch," said Xoana.

Some of the group followed and others dispersed in all directions. They were distracted with all of the activity going on around them in this little village.

Isobel and Harriet were looking at a large fish that was being dragged from a nearby boat. Louis and Samuel were memorised by two tribesmen making sharp arrows. Miss Silverstein and some other parent-helpers walked around keeping a watchful eye on them.

William, Sophie and her dad were hungry so they were focused on Xoana and where she was going. They sat on a grass mat.

"This is a sauce made out of ground and

boiled ants," explained Xoana.

"Yulp!" said Sophie.

"I would never have guessed," said her dad.

This one is grilled monkey and sweet potato," she added and Sophie's dad nodded and swallowed quickly.

William began to cough. '

"Are you ok?" asked Xoana.

"Fine," smiled William drinking his entire glass of water.

"Try this one, grilled toucan," added Xoana moving it towards Sophie.

Sophie put her fork into the dish and quickly took it out. She decided it would be safer to try the fruit instead.

"Mmm!" said Sophie eating some of the fruit salad-like dish. "I'm full," she said not telling the entire truth as she rubbed her stomach.

Some of the group walked around watching the tribes-people go about their daily life, but most of the others sat in the shade exhausted by the heat and humidity. The class gravitated towards the bowls of roasted, round potato chips and cups of chocolate milk.

*   *   *

After the tribes-people had cleaned up, there was some commotion with tribes-men speaking in their own language. Miss Silverstein began to translate. "They are asking us to go with them in their boat to have a look along the river," she explained.

Miss Silverstein politely accepted and the entire group carefully stepped from the river bank onto the long wooden boat. There was enough room for them all to sit down.

The sun had almost set and the birds were noisier than usual as many of the birds were off to sleep. "This was a part of their night-time routine," said one of the tribesmen. The mosquitoes were buzzing about in thick clouds, so the parent-helpers ensured they were protected with insect repellent.

"Look!" said the tribesman, "in the tree to the left are two sloths!"

Miss Silverstein translated. "Sloths spend most of their lives hanging upside-down from tree branches. Their shaggy fur grows downwards, to allow rain to run off them easily" [9]. Algae grows on their fur, and this camouflages them green so they blend in with the trees," [10] said Miss Silverstein.

"Also three-toed sloths can turn their heads up to 270 degrees!" [11]. "I am sure you will agree that sloths are truly amazing creatures!"

The children's attention quickly moved when a tribesman dropped a piece of fish into muddy brown water and a fish feeding frenzy ensued.

A few piranhas had come to the surface and were moving like mad. While this was all happening another tribesmen put another piece of fresh bait on the end of a fishing line and *WHOOP* in seconds he was holding a squirming, live piranha! It was blue-grey in colour, with an amazing set of razor-sharp, pearly-whites!

While the children were fascinated by a live specimen, Miss Silverstein once again took the opportunity to tell them more about this creature.

The tribesman holding the piranha began sharing some information about the fish when suddenly a family of electric eels surprised the class by leaping out of the brown-coloured water. The electric eels began to dance and entertain the class like an acrobatic performance. As the show came to an end, they made their way back to the tribes-people's village.

On the way back they saw a caiman (black alligator) surfacing just above the water line under some dead branches that had fallen into the river. The tribesman shone a torch on its yellow-green eyes, its eyes and mouth reflected in the still brown water.

It was almost completely dark as they approached the village. The tribes-people met them at the river bank with torches and lanterns to help them and guide them safely back to the village.

"It is late and we offer you a place to stay," said the Chief of the Hermities.

"With gratitude, we accept," Miss Silverstein replied.

As William's dad was the last one back to the seating area, Miss Silverstein said "We have had a big day, full of adventure and learning," she smiled. "I think it is best if we stay the night here and hopefully Mrs Bombardo will be found and return tomorrow."

Each group was directed to share a hut with the families of the Hermitie clan. They rested in hammocks covered in mosquito nets as the rainforest noise rang in their ears; it was a soft hum of a multitude of insects and other wildlife. The children were having a lot of fun guessing which sounds belonged to what animals.

This didn't last long, and they were soon fast asleep.

Chapter Nine

In the early morning there was a burst of noise when the tribe returned, singing and dancing as Mrs Bombardo was carried back to where they were eating.

"Mrs Bombardo is back!" yelled Harriet.

Miss Silverstein raced out of her hut. "Mrs Bomb...." is all that would come out of her mouth as she stood there in shock, gobsmacked at the sight of their school principal.

"What is on her face?" whispered Sophie to her dad.

"Face paint of some sort," he replied.

"Nice hair-do, face paint and clothes!" said Louis and with that the whole group laughed hysterically.

Once a nasty principal and now a weird-looking principal, nobody was prepared to say anything but everyone was thinking it. It looked like she had been in a tumble dryer with hair gel, coloured green hairspray and felt tip pens. She looked a mess but she looked unusually happy.

"This is my new look! I have finished with black, I am now into green and brown!" announced Mrs Bombardo.

"Great! Now we have a 'jungle' principal," whispered a William's dad to Harriet's mum.

"It has to be better," Harriet's mum replied. A few children heard, and continued laughing until their stomachs hurt.

Finally finding her voice, "Ok class!" said Miss Silverstein. "We have Mrs Bombardo safely back with us and in a short while we will be heading back to school.

"Look at her hair! Coloured bright green!" added Sophie.

"And... oh my goodness! She's smiling!"

"A rare event!" said William's dad.

In front of their eyes appeared a very different principal, one that was smiling and seemed happier.

Isobel asked Xoana, "What might have happened to her in the jungle?

"It is possible that a ceremony by the elders occurred to ask the bad spirits to leave her and invite the goodness of the green spirits to help her," repliedthe grandmother.

"What are the bad spirits?" asked Sophie.

"The spirits of bad things - jealously, fear and anger." Sophie smiled and nodded as Mrs Bombardo said a usually warm "hello" at the group.

"It is time for us to go back to our huts to pack up and head back to school," said Miss Silverstein.

They all said goodbye to the members of the tribe.

And Miss Silverstein picked up Tappeto ready for a polite and speedy exit.

With that, the tribes-people made a circle and started dancing and singing. Miss Silverstein gave a thank you and farewell speech and they all waved goodbye.

Miss Silverstein promptly laid out Tappeto on some moss and the group sat on the rug. Then the wind changed direction and off and away they went, moving quickly up into the air.

Miss Silverstein's class could be seen smiling and waving goodbye, with Tappeto corner's curved up in the shape of a smile, his tassels waving.

It was a clear day and they could see their huts and spotted a safe place to land. As Tappeto landed briskly yet safely, they were happy to be back together with their group.

Miss Silverstein carefully rolled up Tappeto, and whispered, "Thank you." She then placed him under her arm, as the school group ran off to their huts to pack up their belongings for their journey back to school.

Chapter Ten

The children packed up and it wasn't long before they were all standing with their bags where Miss Silverstein had instructed.

This time the parent-helpers and Mrs Bombardo rolled out Tappeto, getting him ready for their departure.

The children sat on Tappeto and Miss Silverstein once again gave the group the safety briefing... it can be dangerous flying a magic carpet. There are birds to look out for, no windows or doors... just you, the weather and the view!

The entire group knew how fortunate they were to not only ride on a magic carpet but to also go to a wondrous place.

*   *   *

It was a relaxing ride home, watching the view, of the beautiful canopy, the winding river, of flying over the sea to reach land, soaring above the city, and then finally the school playground.

There was no one about, except for the children's parents and a few siblings, excitedly waiting to see their child, brother or sister. Tappeto landed on the grass of the school oval as it made for a great air strip and soft landing.

The parents rushed over, hugging their children and asking about their trip. So delighted were they to see their children, they forgot to mention anything about Tappeto and Mrs Bombardo's new look. However, Miss Silverstein was sure there would be some questions come Monday morning.

Mrs Bombardo looked out of her office window and smiled as she spotted Miss Silverstein with Tappeto rolled up under her arm, walking out of the school gate.

References

[1] Oddizzi, *Rainforests. Canopy Layer for primary kids.*
Accessed on: May 3, 2019. [Online]. Available:
https://www.oddizzi.com/teachers/explore-the-world/
physical- features/ecosystems/rainforests/rainforest-layers/
canopy-layer/

[2] Oddizzi, *Rainforests. Canopy Layer for primary kids.*
Accessed on: May 3, 2019. [Online]. Available:
https://www.oddizzi.com/teachers/explore-the-world/
physical-features/ecosystems/rainforests/rainforest-layers/
canopy-layer/

[3] National Geographic Kids, *10 Amazing Amazon Facts!*
Accessed on: April 30, 2019. [Online]. Available:
https://www.natgeokids.com/au/discover/geography/
physical-geography/amazon-facts/

[4] National Geographic Kids, *10 Amazing Amazon Facts!*
Accessed on: April 30, 2019. [Online]. Available:
https://www.natgeokids.com/au/discover/geography/
physical-geography/amazon-facts/

[5] National Geographic Kids, *10 Amazing Amazon Facts!*
Accessed on: April 30, 2019. [Online]. Available:
https://www.natgeokids.com/au/discover/geography/
physical-geography/amazon-facts/

[6] National Geographic Kids, *10 Amazing Amazon Facts!*
Accessed on: April 30, 2019. [Online]. Available:
https://www.natgeokids.com/au/discover/geography/
physical-geography/amazon-facts/

[7]   National Geographic Kids, *10 Amazing Amazon Facts!*
      Accessed on: April 30, 2019. [Online]. Available:
      https://www.natgeokids.com/au/discover/geography/
      physical-geography/amazon-facts/

[8]   Dixon, D. 2018, *Australian Geographic The Atlas of Animals
      Mapping Earth s Wildlife*
      Weldon Owen imprint of Kings Road Publishing, London.

[9]   National Geographic Kids, *10 Amazing Amazon Facts!*
      Accessed on: April 30, 2019. [Online]. Available:
      https://www.natgeokids.com/au/discover/geography/
      physical-geography/amazon-facts/

[10] A. Bradford, *Live Science, Sloths: The World s Slowest
      Mammal,* Nov. 26, 2018.
      Accessed on: May 2, 2019. [Online]. Available:
      https://www.livescience.com/27612-sloths.html

[11] A. Bradford, *Live Science, Sloths: The World s Slowest
      Mammal,* Nov. 26, 2018.
      Accessed on: May 2, 2019. [Online]. Available:
      https://www.livescience.com/27612-sloths.html

About the Author

Kristina is a children's book author who is passionate about children's literacy and education.

Kristina holds a Diploma of Teaching (Primary), Bachelor of Education (Primary) and a Masters of Education (Teaching English to Speakers of Other Languages). She works as a Language and Learning Advisor at RMIT University and in her own business as a publisher and publishing consultant.

Kristina enjoys being around people, especially children, and listening to their stories. She lives in Melbourne, Australia with her husband and two daughters.

Kristina has always loved to write and spends many hours writing, reading, watching and listening for ideas. She carries a small notebook and pen with her to 'catch' ideas before they evaporate. Her wonderful ideas can come from anywhere at any time!

Lightning Source UK Ltd.
Milton Keynes UK
UKHW020805200721
387465UK00015B/2455

9 780994 273857